Superphonics® *Storybooks* **will help your child to learn to read using Ruth Miskin's highly effective phonic method. Each story is fun to read and has been carefully written to include particular sounds and spellings.**

The Storybooks are graded so your child can progress with confidence from easy words to harder ones. There are four levels - Blue (the easiest), Green, Purple and Turquoise (the hardest). Each level is linked to one of the core *Superphonics® Books.*

ISBN: 978 0 340 79703 7

Text copyright © 2002 Gill Munton
Illustrations copyright © 2002 Guy Parker-Rees

Editorial by Gill Munton
Design by Sarah Borny

The rights of Gill Munton and Guy Parker-Rees to be identified as the author and illustrator of this Work have been asserted by them in accordance with the Copyright, Designs and Patents Act 1988.

First published in Great Britain 2002

10 9 8 7 6 5 4 3

First published in ... ...s Books,
a division of Hachette Children's Books,
338 Euston Road, London NW1 3BH
An Hachette UK Company. www.hachette.co.uk
Printed and bound in China by WKT Company Ltd.
A CIP record is registered by and held at the British Library.

Target words

All the Green Storybooks focus on the following sounds:

Double consonants, e.g. **ll** as in **yell**	Blended consonants, e.g. **ng** as in **hang**

Two or three consonants together, e.g. **sk** as in **skin**, **ft** as in **lift**

These target words are featured in the book:

all	kiss	bricks	socks
biff	kisses	brushing	sticks
biggest	less	dusting	suck
calls	mess	fangs	swing
cress	shell	hang	things
cross	well	hatch	tucked
dolls	yell	kick	
eggs		lick	and
Fusspot	along	long	basket
grass	back	neck	blanket
hill	black	rocks	book-
hiss	blocks	sing	shelf

bronto	from	must	stand
brush	grunt	nest	thump
bump	honk	pants	twigs
clip	kinds	pink	vests
crunch	just	rest	
crusts	lift	skin	
dents	milk	splash	
dust	munch	stamp	

(Words containing sounds and spellings practised in the Blue Storybooks have been used in the stories, too.)

Other words

Also included are some common words (e.g. **her**, **their**) which your child will be learning in his or her first few years at school.

A few other words have been used to help the stories to flow.

Reading the book

1 Make sure you and your child are sitting in a quiet, comfortable place.

2 Tell him or her a little about the stories, without giving too much away:

In the first story, a new puppy makes a terrible mess!

In the second story, we meet some dinosaur babies.

This will give your child a mental picture; having a context for a story makes it easier to read the words.

3 Read the target words (above) together. This will mean that you can both enjoy the stories without having to spend too much time working out the words. Help your child to sound out each word (e.g. **l-o-ng**) before saying the whole word.

4 Let your child read the stories aloud. Help him or her with any difficult words and discuss the stories as you go along. Stop now and again to ask your child to predict what will happen next. This will help you to see whether he or she has understood what has happened so far.

Above all, enjoy the stories, and praise your child's reading!

Ruth Miskin's
Superphonics ®

Green Storybook

Fiona Fusspot

by Gill Munton

Illustrated by Guy Parker-Rees

Hodder
Children's
Books

a division of Hachette Children's Books

Fiona Fusspot

Fiona Fusspot
In long pink socks,

Books on the bookshelf,
Dolls in a box,

Her dad (Mr. Fusspot)

Down on his knees,

Brushing the grass,

And dusting the trees,

Fiona Fusspot,

Six today!

What's in the basket?

Who's come to play?

Lift off the blanket,

Lift him up,

A big wet kiss

From a little black pup!

Fiona Fusspot
Tucked up tight,
Her dad (Mr. Fusspot)
Kisses her goodnight,

But little black puppy

Is up and about,

Runs along the rug,

And runs in and out,

Bits in the bath tub,

Mud on the mat,

Dents in the back door ...

"Just look at that!"
Calls Mr. Fusspot,
Very cross and red,

Little black puppy
Just sits in his bed,

Fiona Fusspot
Gives him a kiss,
"It's the biggest mess
  I've ever seen!

But ...

... I like it like this!"

Bronto babies

Bronto babies hatch from their eggs,

And hang the shells on bronto pegs,

And stamp along on bronto legs,

Bronto babies suck their thumbs,

And bump along on little pink tums,

And grunt, like piglets,

for their mums,

Bronto babies munch on cress,

And lick their milk up

  (more or less),

And make a cressy, milky mess,

Bronto babies crunch their crusts,

And splash their skin

with water and dust,

Bronto bubble bath is a must,

Bronto babies stand at the well,

And brush their fangs

with a bit of old shell,

And clip their nails

with a hiss and a yell,

Bronto babies play with bricks,

And blocks and rocks

and twigs and sticks,

They bump and thump

and biff and kick,

Bronto babies honk and sing,

They sing about all kinds of things,

Bronto parties go with a swing,

Bronto babies have a rest

In bronto pants and bronto vests,

Hush! All tucked up

in the bronto nest,

Bronto babies -
  but where can they be?
At the top of the hill,
  or up in the tree?
Where have they gone?
  I wish I could see
A bronto leg, or a neck,
  or a knee ...

Bronto babies!

Here they come!

But ...

... they've grown up
into bronto mums!

And bronto dads
with BIG pink tums!